Smokey

written and illustrated by

BILL PEET

HOUGHTON MIFFLIN COMPANY BOSTON

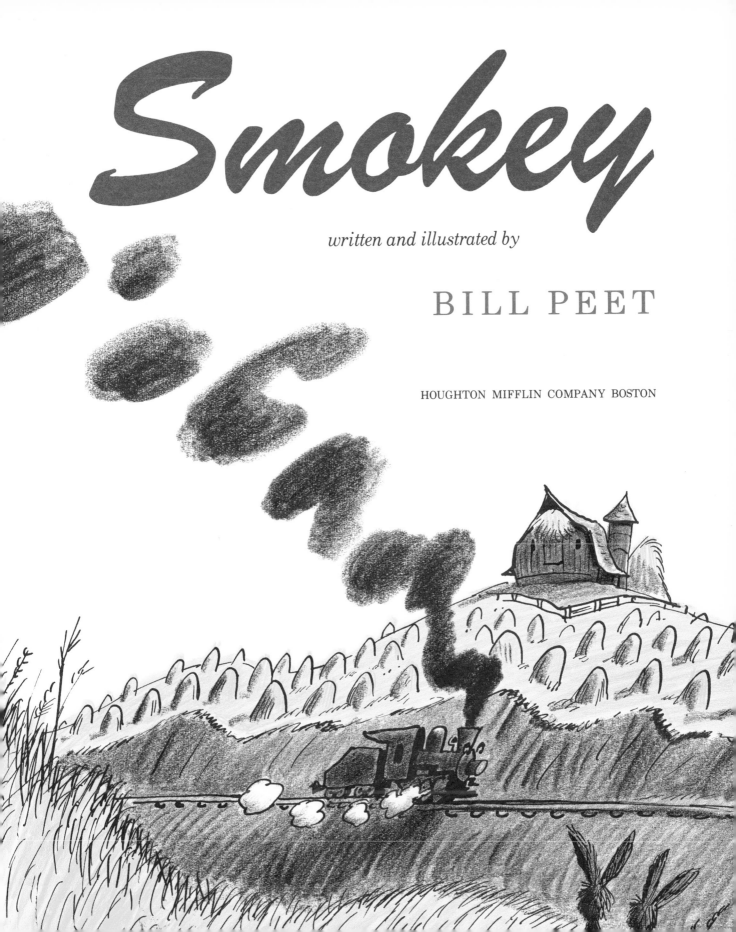

Old Smokey for many long years had worked hard
Switching the freight cars around in the yard.
He wheezed and he huffed and he puffed and he chugged,
No matter how tired he pulled and he tugged,

Backward and forward, forward and back,
And all of the time on the very same track

Lining up freight cars for day after day
So the big diesel engines could haul them away.

When he'd switched the last car and his work was all through,
With no place to go and with nothing to do,
He would sit on the loneliest part of the track
Blowing smoke rings like daydreams from out of his stack.
He would watch them go drifting away through the air
And wish that he too might be going somewhere.

The big diesels stopped in the yard now and then
And bragged about all of the places they'd been,

While Smokey would listen to all the details
Of their fabulous trips on the silvery rails.

He imagined himself at the head of a train
Speeding along over mountain and plain,
Tearing through tunnels as black as the night
Then out over trestles of dizzying height.
He traveled along through his wonderful dream
Till it faded from sight like a big puff of steam.
Then he sighed in despair. There was no place to go
With a rumbling long line of freight cars in tow.

One morning poor Smokey just happened to hear
Some news that surprised him and filled him with fear.
"Did you know?" a big sleeping car said with a yawn.
"Old Smokey's all through. Next week he'll be gone.
They finally got sick of his dirty black smoke,
And not only that; he's an awful slowpoke."
"I think that's a shame," said a nice old caboose.
"It's the junkyard for him, if he has no more use."

Smokey knew of the place for he'd passed there one day
And seen the old engines all rusting away.
Mighty Mo and Big Louie and Old Ninety-Nine
And big Hercules of the North Central Line.
They had simply worn out and had nothing to do.
Their travels were over and now they were through.

"Well, there's one thing," said Smokey, "that I'm going to do.
I'm taking a trip, and a good long one, too."
So he crept behind boxcars along a side track
Until he sneaked up by the train watchman's shack.

The watchman was reading a new comic book
And didn't give Smokey so much as a look
As he huffed and he puffed and went steaming by
On out of the freight yard as easy as pie.

"I'm free," said old Smokey, "there's no need to hurry.
When I puff clouds of smoke now I don't have to worry."
But nearby on a hilltop, strangely enough,
Someone was watching and counting each puff.
"What's it say? What's the word, chief?" said Little Wolf Ears.
"We haven't received a smoke signal for years."
"It's the worst sort of insult," said Chief Crazy Hawk,
"And we're not going to stand for that kind of smoke talk."

So they went roaring off in their old Hupmobile,
Whooping and yelling with the chief at the wheel.
They raced down the road alongside of the track,
Then with spears and with arrows they launched their attack.
Smokey turned on the steam and picked up the pace
And away they all went in a wild screaming chase.
But Smokey, alas, was in no shape to run.
In less than a mile he was nearly all done.

The braves were all set to close in for the kill
When they screamed to a stop at the top of a hill,
For a wagon was there with a big load of hay,
And Smokey went puffing on safely away.

By now he was just about dead in his tracks
So he stopped in a woods to cool off and relax
And give his poor run-down old wheels a good rest
Before he continued his journey out West.
Soon after sundown he heard an owl hoot
Or could it perhaps be a train-whistle toot?

Then through the woods shot a long flash of light—
A fast freight came roaring down out of the night.

Smokey took off just as fast as he could,
Racing at top speed away through the wood.
He wasn't so worried about his own neck,
He was much more afraid that he'd cause a train wreck.

So he jumped off the track and plunged over a bank
With a bumpity, clunkity, clinkity, clank!
Wheels over cab with a crunch and a crash
Then finally a great big ker-ploppity splash.

Early next day about quarter to nine
A furious farmer called the North Central line.
"I've put up with your noisy trains year after year
A hootin' and tootin' and roarin' past here,
But you'll not make my duck pond a junky old dump
For broken-down engines," complained the old grump.
"So get the thing out of here, pretty quick too,
Or I'll call up the sheriff, that's just what I'll do."

So the North Central line sent a big railroad crane
And hauled out the muddy and soggy old train.
And then came a diesel to push Smokey back,
And they left him to sit at the end of the track.

Now he was done for, no doubt about that,
His smokestack was crushed like a battered old hat.
It was so out of shape that he couldn't blow rings
But strangely enough he could blow other things,
Big figure eights and sixes and twos,
Capital letters and big curlicues.

His letters which just about filled the whole sky
Were seen by a teacher, Miss Adelaide Fry.
She was on her way back from a summer vacation
And had just left her train at the North Central Station.
"Amazing!" she cried, "why that's really stupendous!
It's supercolossal—and also tremendous.
That little old engine's the best I've seen yet
For teaching my pupils the whole alphabet."
So she went to the school board and they soon agreed
That Miss Fry's new idea was a good one indeed
And the railroad, it turned out, was happy to settle
For what the old engine was worth in scrap metal.

At the school they put Smokey outside in the yard
Where the children got busy and worked extra hard.
They scraped off the rust, pounded out every dent
Except for his smokestack and that was left bent.
Then they painted him up to look better than new,
Bright red and deep yellow and robin's-egg blue.

Smokey learned all the letters, and not only that,
He spelled simple words such as "mother" and "cat."
Oh, he sometimes forgets to cross all of his T's
And a few of the letters get lost in the breeze,
But the children are learning much faster and better
As they watch with delight every big Smokey letter.
They come to the school bright and early each day
Then when classes are over they all want to stay.

This new teaching system the children love so
Is called "choo-choo training" . . . now wouldn't you know?